pocket.watch
RYAN'S MYSTERY PLAYDATE

It's a
MARVELOUS
MYSTERY!

W9-AAU-922

SIMON SPOTLIGHT

An imprint of Simon & Schuster Children's Publishing Division • New York London Toronto Sydney New Delhi
1230 Avenue of the Americas, New York, New York 10020 • This Simon Spotlight edition January 2020
Text by May Nakamura • TM & © 2020 PocketWatch, Inc. & Hour Hand Productions, LLC. All Rights Reserved. Ryan's Mystery Playdate and all related titles, logos, and
characters, and the pocket.watch logo, are trademarks of PocketWatch, Inc. All other rights are the property of their respective owners. • Stock photos by iStock
For more information about special discounts for bulk purchases, please contact Simon & Schuster Special Sales at 1-866-506-1949 or business@simonandschuster.com.
Manufactured in the United States of America 1119 LAK
2 4 6 8 10 9 7 5 3 1
ISBN 978-1-5344-6241-0

Hi. It's me, Ryan! I have a playdate coming over today. Do you want to play too?

There's one thing, though—I don't know who my playdate is! In order to find out, I need to complete challenges and earn hints about my playdate's identity.

Flip to the very end of the book and carefully punch out the play pieces from the cardstock sheet. You'll use these to help me complete the challenges.

What are we waiting for? It's time to solve the mystery!

Watch your step!

To earn our first hint, we have to travel from one island to another island. Sounds easy, right? Not if . . . **THE FLOOR IS LAVA!**

We'll need to walk on special lava-resistant rocks to safely cross to the other side. Place the rocks and create a path connecting the two islands.

Phew! We were able to safely cross the lava floor. And look what's waiting for us on the island: the first hint!

The hint is a deck of cards. A lot of people play with cards, even my daddy! But Daddy can't be my mystery playdate . . . can he? Let's look for another hint!

This next challenge is called "**Eye on the Pie**," and it's going to be sweet. We have to put a pie-whipped cream and all-onto Daddy's face. Aim well, and don't miss! Place the pie onto Daddy's face.

I'm ready whenever you are!

Wow, look at the yummy mess we've made! Whipped cream looks great on Daddy, don't you think?

It's time to release the Mystery Splasher for our second hint.

The hint is a rabbit. Maybe the mystery playdate is a zookeeper . . . who likes to play cards?

I think we need one more hint to solve the mystery of the secret playdate.

The third and last hint is locked inside a mystery box. How do you think it opens? First let's try knocking on the box three times.

Knock, knock, knock!

Look, that opened up a drawer! There's a red key and a green key inside. I bet these will help us open the box.

Place the green key on the green knob and the red key on the red knob to unlock the box.

Ta-da! We unlocked our third hint! It is a **black hat**.

So, our three hints are: **cards, rabbit,** and **hat.**
Have you solved the mystery of my playdate? I think I have a guess.
It's time to find out if we're correct!

Huh? The Mystery Guest Box is empty. Is my playdate . . . a **ghost**?

Whoa, my mystery playdate appeared out of thin air! He is . . .

Murray the Magician!

Have you ever seen a magician perform at a circus, at a birthday party, or maybe on TV? I have a feeling that this playdate is going to be full of amazing tricks!

Murray brought presents for all of us. Thank you, Murray!
Mommy got a colorful pinwheel, and I got a bag of yummy cookies that we can share.

Daddy's present was a bowling ball! How did something that big and heavy fit in Murray's thin briefcase?

It's magic!

Now it's time for a marvelous playdate! I want to show you a magic trick that Murray taught me. Are you ready?

Look closely. I have a cup in my hand, and Daddy has a water bottle. Daddy pours all the water into my cup.

Now it's your turn. Wave the wand over the cup. When you wave it, don't forget to say the magic word:

"ABRACADABRA!"

Thank you for joining me on my magical playdate. I hope I see you again soon!

Turn the page to learn a marvelous magic trick!

BUILD YOUR OWN MAGIC TRICK BOX!

Build this easy and fun magic trick box with a grown-up. When you place items inside this magic box, they'll magically "disappear." Wow!

How to build it:

• Punch out the pieces labeled Box A, B, and C in the back of the book.
• Lay the pieces down in front of you. For Boxes B and C, Ryan should be facing up. For Box A, Ryan should be facing down.
• For Boxes B and C, fold the black tabs up and in toward the center. Then fold the green tabs in. Fold the blue tabs up and over the black tabs. Tuck the flaps into the slits to secure everything in place.
• For Box A, fold up both sides, leaving the green tab in the middle. Tuck in the blue tab with a star on it. Now you should have the shape of the box. Fold in the black tabs. Then fold and tuck the remaining blue tabs.
• Place Box B inside Box C. Make sure that Ryan's head is pointing the same way on both boxes.
• Slide both boxes, head first, into Box A. Now you're finished building the magic box!

How to perform the magic trick:

• Slide open the box so you can see the inside of Box B (the top box).
• Ask a friend or family member to place an item inside.
• Close the box and tell them to say "Abracadabra!"
• Pinch the starred corners of the box with one hand, and slowly pull open the box with your other hand. The empty bottom box (Box C) will open, while the top box with the item inside will stay closed.
• Say, "Wow, your item disappeared! It's magic!" Then take a bow!